1. Grab a grandma
2. Make sure that blind bat has her magnifying glass
3. Spot the idiot you idiot!

AHS
EAGLES
TEXAS

ALLEN EAGLES

SAVEMONEY
SAVEMONEY
SAVEMONEY

SAVEMONEY
SAVEMONEY
SAVEMONEY

Jaylen

Giro d'Italia
ESTATHÉ
VERONA
ESTA
ESTATHÉ

zetta dello Sport
il rosa della vita
Uscita
Giro d'Italia

UNION
UNION

NO
PARKING
CONG. JERRY P. TREÑAS
MAYOR JOE III ESPINOSA
BOYSEN The No. 1 PAINT
NO
PARKING
HUMBLE
THYSELF
adidas
SAN FRA

YO!

Printed in Great Britain
by Amazon

72510437R00015